Illustrations: Ann de Bode
Original title: *Waar is mama?*
© Van In, Lier, 1997. Van In Publishers, Grote Markt 39,
2500 Lier, Belgium.
© in this edition Evans Brothers Limited 1999
(world English rights excluding the USA and Canada)
English text by Su Swallow

First published in Great Britain by
Evans Brothers Limited
2A Portman Mansions
Chiltern Street
London W1M 1LE

Printed in Belgium by Hendrix

0 237 51 953 4

HELPING HANDS

MUMMY, MUMMY, WHERE ARE YOU?

ANN DE BODE AND RIEN BROERE

Evans

Evans Brothers Limited

One day, Jessie went shopping with her mum.
They went in and out of shops all day long,
until Jessie was really tired.
'I want to go home. My feet hurt.'
'Just a bit longer,' said Mum.
'I want to look at the books on the first floor.'
So they went up on the escalator.

Mum started looking at the books.
Jessie didn't mind.
She liked looking at books, too.
She sat down on the floor and started to read.
Soon, Mum came to find her.
What a pity. It was an exciting story!

'Can we go now?' asked Jessie
as they got to the escalator to go down.
But Jessie's mum stopped.
'Just a minute,' she said.
'I want to have a quick look at those jackets.
You don't mind, do you?'

Jessie sighed and followed her mum.
Wherever she looked, there were clothes,
lots of clothes. Clothes for grown-ups,
in rather dull colours.
Why don't grown-ups wear bright
colours? thought Jessie.
I wonder what Mum would look like in a
green skirt, a yellow blouse and red shoes!

Jessie was bored so she hid behind some sweaters.
This is fun! she thought. No one can see me now.
And I can make the rail spin round,
and no one knows why the clothes are moving.
But she'd soon had enough of that game.
Surely Mum had finished by now?
Jessie decided to go and find her.

But where was Mum? Jessie looked round.
Where had she last seen Mum?
By the jackets? Or by the shirts? Jessie couldn't
remember, and all the rails looked the same.
I'm not afraid, thought Jessie.
I am not afraid. I must just have a good
look round.

Jessie looked everywhere, but there was no sign of Mum.
She must have found something
very pretty, thought Jessie.
When Mum's looking at clothes, it can take hours.
Perhaps she was trying something on?
Jessie peeped under the fitting room curtains.
At the third one, Jessie smiled.
Those were Mum's shoes, weren't they?

Jessie pulled the curtain back.
A lady she didn't know glared at her.
'Sorry,' cried Jessie. 'I thought you were my mum.'
She let go of the curtain, and
looked back at the clothes rails.
What a lot of mothers!
But Jessie's mum was not among them.
Jessie began to feel afraid.

She started dashing about looking for Mum.
She ran so hard she got out of breath.
Suddenly, at the top of the escalator,
Jessie realised what must have happened.
When Mum couldn't see me, she thought,
she must have gone down
to wait for me at the exit.

But there wasn't just one exit.
There were four of them!
Jessie hadn't thought of that.
She went to the first exit. No Mum.
Jessie tried not to worry.
But still no Mum at the second or third exits.
Now Jessie started to feel really worried.
One exit to go. Oh dear, Mum wasn't there either.

Jessie turned back into the store.
She ran through the perfume department,
full of bottles and powders.
They smelt nice, but not the same as Mum.
Jessie felt scared.
She bumped into a pair of legs.
'Hey!' shouted the legs. 'Look where you're going!'
But Jessie didn't hear. She'd lost her mum.

Jessie hurried about for a few more minutes.
Then, at last, she stopped.
She was tired and her feet really hurt now.
She was feeling very upset and
was trying not to cry.
She didn't notice the people round her.
She just kept thinking about her mum.
Mummy, Mummy, where are you?

Suddenly, Jessie felt a hand on her shoulder.
Mum! she thought, and looked round.
But it was a man she didn't know.
'What's the matter, little girl?' he asked.
His voice was deep and rather loud.
Jessie wanted to answer, but the words
   got stuck in her throat.
'I - I've lost - lost my mum,' she whispered.

'Don't worry,' said the man. 'I'll help you.'
But Jessie remembered what her parents
had always said:
'Never go with strangers, no matter
how kind they seem!'
So Jessie pulled away and ran off.
She went towards the exit,
but she was sure the man was following her.

She pushed her way through the revolving door
and out into the fresh air.
She ran down the street, not
knowing where she was going.
The man mustn't catch up with her!
She kept running until she was out of breath.
Then she stopped and looked back.
Thank goodness! He was nowhere to be seen.

But her relief didn't last long.
She suddenly realised that she
had no idea where she was.
There were tall buildings all around,
and noisy traffic, and people
talking to each other. And she was all alone.

Suddenly, Jessie saw a policeman on
the other side of the road.
He would be able to help her.
She shouted and waved, but he didn't hear her.
So she had to cross the road.
　　　A car stopped and the driver waved her across.

'Mr Policeman!' shouted Jessie. 'Help, Mr Policeman!'
She had to run to catch up with him.
Finally, he turned round.
'I...I...' said Jessie, panting. 'I'm...I've...'
'Slow down!' said the man, smiling.
'Get your breath back and then tell me what's the matter.'
Jessie breathed slowly and deeply.
'Mr Policeman, I've lost my mum.'

'I'm not a real policeman, you know,' the man said.
'I'm a security guard. But I can still help you.
Where did you lose your mum?'
But Jessie didn't know the answer to that question.
'It was in a big store,' she said.
'There were lots of clothes, and an escalator,
and some books.'

'Well, now,' said the man.
'That could be a bit of a problem.
There are lots of shops like that round here.
Shall I tell you what we're going to do?
First, we'll go to my office, it's very near.
Then we'll see what to do next.'

The security guard's office looked a bit like a shop.
There was a counter in the middle,
and two ladies working behind it.
'This little girl has lost her mum,' said the man.
'Can one of you look after her for a little while?
I'm going to ring all the stores.'
And he asked Jessie for her name and address.
At least she knew the answer to that question!

One of the ladies came from behind the counter.
She had a soft voice and a kind smile.
'Come along,' she said. 'Let's go in the room next door.
We can wait in there, and have something to drink.
Are you thirsty?'
Jessie nodded. Yes, she was very thirsty.

It was a nice room, with plants, and comfortable chairs.
There was even a television in one corner.
The lady brought a drink and some biscuits.
'Now, tell me what happened,' she said.
So Jessie told her everything.
Even about the man who frightened her.
   'I understand why you were frightened,' she laughed.
'but I'm sure he only wanted to help you.'

The other lady came in.
She was holding a huge teddy bear.
It was nearly as big as Jessie.
'This is Mr Brown,' she said.
'He's our lucky mascot.
I think he would like to stay with you for a bit.
So you can wait for your mum together.'

'How are you going to find my mum?' asked Jessie.
'We'll call all the stores,' explained the lady.
'We'll tell them your name and what you look like.
They will make an announcement
to say you are waiting here
for your mum to collect you.'
Good, thought Jessie. Now I just have to wait.

'We must get back to work,' said the lady,
'but I'll put the television on for you.'
There was a funny cartoon, which made Jessie laugh.
She even forgot where she was,
and didn't see anyone come in -
someone she had been looking for for a long time.

'So!' said Mum. 'This is where you've been!
Eating biscuits and watching television. Very nice!'
Jessie ran up to her mum, who hugged her tight.
'You should have stayed close to me!' said Mum.
She pretended to be cross, but she wasn't really.
There were tears in her eyes, but not
because she was angry.

The nice lady came to sit next to them.
She gave Mum a cup of coffee,
and Jessie some more biscuits.
'So,' she said, 'it's all turned out ok.'
'It certainly has,' said Mum with a sigh.
'If only you knew how scared I was!'
'I'm sure you were,' said the lady.
     'But can I offer you a bit of advice?'

'It's easy to get lost in a big store,' said the lady.
'It's a good idea to agree where
to meet if you lose each other.
And if you lose your mummy, Jessie,
just ask one of the sales ladies.
She will help you.'
Jessie promised to do just that,
but she had no intention of losing her mum ever again.

'We'd better get home now,' said Mum.
She shook hands with everyone, and
thanked them over and over again.
'Don't you have something to say, too?'
she asked Jessie.
'Yes, thank you from me too,' said Jessie.
'I'm never going to lose Mum again!'
'Good!' said the lady with a smile. 'I'm counting on you!'

Jessie and her mum started to leave.
Jessie suddenly stopped and went back to the counter.
'I'm sorry, I forgot to give you Mr Brown back.'
'You see, he brought you luck,' said the lady.
'Bye, bye, kind bear,' said Jessie,
and gave him a big kiss on the nose.
'A big thank you to you, too!'